A Trip to the Moon

It is a lovely sunny day, and George and his friend Edmond Elephant are playing with their space toys in the garden.

Oh dear! Edmond's space toy has landed
on Peppa's head. She is not happy.
"Are you going to the moon, boys?" asks Daddy Pig.
"Moon!" says George.
"It's just boring space stuff for babies,
Daddy," says Peppa. "It's not real."
"Space *is* real, Peppa," replies Daddy Pig.

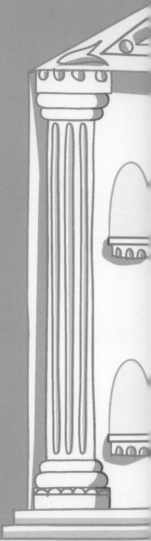

Mummy Pig tells everyone there is a show
at the museum that is all about the moon.
"That sounds fun! Shall we go and
see it?" asks Daddy Pig.
George and Edmond laugh.
They want to see the show.

Hee! Hee!

At the museum, they all buy tickets.
"Are we really going to the moon?" Peppa asks.
"No, Peppa, it's just pretend," Miss Rabbit tells her.

Mr Rabbit is the tour guide.
"This way for our trip to the moon!" he calls,
leading them inside. "Prepare for blast-off!"

When they are all seated in the rocket,
a voice booms, "Blast off!"
"We live on a planet. Does anyone know
what it's called?" Mr Rabbit asks.
"Earth?" Daddy Pig guesses.
"That's right!" Mr Rabbit smiles.

"And what is the moon made of?"
Mr Rabbit wants to know next.
"The moon is made of cheese,
of course!" Daddy Pig jokes.
But Mr Rabbit doesn't find it very funny.
"No, the moon is made of rock. This is
a serious tour, so no jokes, please!"

"It is *pretend* though, isn't it?" Peppa asks. "Yes, Peppa. If it was the real moon, you could jump over my head!" Mr Rabbit tells her. "Gravity is what keeps us on the ground, and it is weaker on the moon, so you can jump higher."

Some big rubber bands drop down,
and Mr Rabbit straps everyone in.
Peppa and the others feel like they are
jumping on the moon. It is so much fun!
Miss Rabbit tells them to say
"Moon cheese!" as she takes a picture.

It is the end of the tour,
so Miss Rabbit takes everyone
to the moon shop.

"How about some real moon cheese?" says Miss Rabbit.
"How much is it?" asks Daddy Pig.

"Five pounds, please," says Miss Rabbit.
"Five pounds?" snorts Daddy Pig.
"It's all for a good cause,"
says Miss Rabbit.

"I like the moon now because it's very interesting!" says Peppa, holding a picture of everybody bouncing on the moon. "And very tasty!" laughs Daddy Pig, eating his yummy moon cheese.